THE CRY
OF THE
LITTLE ROSES

Prophecies and Prayers about Human Trafficking

LORENE MASTERS

DEDICATION

To:

Kelly Rose Patterson, whose survival inspires hope for all the fallen Roses, and shows that they, too, can bloom filled with love and purpose, proclaiming that healing is achievable for everyone.

And to my Lord and Savior Jesus Christ, who embodies Love Crucified Arose, the beautiful Rose of Sharon, constantly granting life to the dead and broken, and calling forth those things that do not exist as though they do.

CONTENTS

INTRODUCTION

This book was created at God's request. I accepted this calling and was led to a quiet place where I could truly listen to His voice. There, He began to unveil the messages that would fill the pages that follow, in a supernatural way.

I write this book not for human acknowledgment, but to intercede with the hope of shattering the demonic stronghold in the spiritual realm that seeks to harm both children and women, including those yet to be born. With sincere intercession, I express these thoughts in the hope that Jesus sends mighty angels to comfort His daughters, little Roses born from His love. These Roses are meant to thrive and spread joy and love around the world. Their cries grow increasingly urgent as the world turns away, indifferent to their plight.

Soon, the temporary god of this age will overpower those who support the horrors of child sex trafficking, causing callouses of indifference to form over their hearts as they engage in works of darkness. This hardening of the heart is already evident in those who kill and promote the murder of unborn babies, as well as in those who profit from the sale of children through human trafficking. Jesus sees, hears, and His heart is breaking.

Will you become part of the community of intercessors? Many have lingered in the shadows over the years, observing and praying for what burdens the Lord. Will you pray? Will you dare to enter the cover of night when shadows fall and peril surrounds? Will you proceed without needing human praise, instead only desiring God's approval? Will you pray for their angels to be sent forth to save them? If you say yes, thank you! If you cannot go, then don't stop praying that the little Roses will know the face of their Savior when they are welcomed into their eternal home.

PART I
HE SEES

Come now. Come to the garden,

for He is there waiting for all who will say yes.

He will strengthen you, heal you,

and help you to help the forgotten in His name.

He sees.

Come and listen to His heart. Strive to hear His voice.

Come. He is calling.

The little Roses are waiting for you.

The eyes of the Lord are in every place,
Watching the evil and the good.
Proverbs 15:3

THE GARDEN

Long ago, in a beautiful, idyllic garden, our mother, Eve, made a grave, life-altering mistake. In those days, before the Fall, the garden was a source of life, free of pain and tears. However, with the arrival of sin due to disobedience, humanity has turned against one another. In selfishness and lust, they harmed the littlest of us, leaving these little Roses of God's heart in such profound pain that no human can completely alleviate. They suffer in solitude, with broken hearts yearning for the safety and joy that the garden once provided, yet for the most part, their cries remain unanswered. The little ones' garden has been desecrated. Few venture through the gate, searching for the little Roses destroyed by powerful men in black boots, who crush the fragile blooms. Evil women who despise these children view them merely as a product to be exploited and discarded. Nevertheless, God continues to call for the descendants of Adam and Eve, urging them to come, to witness, and to rescue those who cannot save themselves. Yet most do not hear. They are preoccupied with their lives, accumulating more gardens, homes, food, and possessions to satiate themselves in their brief, meager existence on earth. They forget and care little that another world awaits, where they must answer for their actions in His name for the little ones.

See that you do not despise one of these little ones, for I tell you that their angels in Heaven always see the face of my Father in Heaven.

Matthew 18:10

Mothers

I dreamt I was in an apartment with two lovely girls. One was my daughter, safe and sound; the other, not mine, was in her room where dreadful events were about to occur. This poor child would never recover. A man with an evil black heart stood in her bedroom, which was cluttered with clothes meant to be packed for an anticipated trip. No one seemed to care about the impending danger she faced. Her mother knew about it and chose not to act; she was complicit. She had sold her daughter to the highest bidder. Consumed by fear of what was to happen, I placed my daughter in my room to protect her. The other girl, only 12, had no one to come to her aid. I attempted to assist her, but I woke up just then, overwhelmed by terror.

The Lord spoke to my heart, and He is appalled that this was happening! I fell to my knees feeling helpless. All I could do was pray for mothers whose children are safe in their beds, shielded from harm. I prayed that they would awaken and advocate for children who have no one to save them, no one to pray for them. These innocent flowers are being damaged and crushed. They need rescuing so they can grow and live in safety. Will it be you?

Can a mother forget the baby at her breast and have no compassion on the child she has borne? Though she may forget, I will not forget you!
Isaiah 49:15

WHO IS TENDING THE ROSES?

I see two beautiful little girls swimming in a hotel pool. A man is watching them—a stranger with ill motives. He desires to kidnap them and quickly put them in his car. He will pull out their little flowers and tender stems, trampling and destroying them. Then, when he is done, he will deliver them and collect the money promised. He is a fool! For God sees! And He is adding wrath to the arsenal of eternal punishment.

Where are the mothers? The fathers? Who is watching the little Roses as they play in innocence? As they laugh with unhindered joy? Why does no one see? What about the other adults? Why does no one intervene?

O Father, release mighty warring angels on behalf of the little flowers who are left alone in a cruel, sinful world! Send them now! Wake up the mothers, the fathers, and the caregivers to the plight of the little ones who have no one to protect them. I pray that all of us will be aware of what is going on.

May we all pray for divine intervention so that our eyes, hearts, and minds will be sensitive to those who have motives from the pit of Hell. I pray for a strong angelic presence around these innocent ones who aren't being tended to by a parent or guardian. O Father! Come quickly to their aid! Please show them your face! And may it not be too late.

See, I am sending an angel ahead of you to guard you along the way and to bring you to the place I have prepared.
Exodus 23:20

DIRTY MONEY

I observe a large, overweight man with a protruding belly and a small head, enormous legs, and tiny feet, walking with malicious intent. Despite his purposeful gait, he strides not toward the Kingdom of Heaven, but to the Horrors of Hell. Paper money falls from his pockets, pants, and shirt, while dirty bills also peek from under his hat, protrude from his shoes, and litter the ground. This grotesque man accelerates his pace. Bills start to swirl in the wind, landing on others who eagerly grab them and flee. Each bill features the image of a little girl. The flow of money increases rapidly for all who possess it. They run as if pursued by the hounds of Hell. People from various backgrounds snatch up the cash like a rabid dog aware of its impending fate. They quickly seek refuge in alleyways and dark passages, gathering in shadowy rooms. The amount of cash surges as the values on the bills escalate. However, despite the influx, their greed remains unquenched. Money accumulates in piles on a filthy table. Liquor spills over the funds; they wipe their faces with it. They even resort to using it as toilet paper due to the abundance. It has become worthless cash. Yet their insatiable lust and greed persist. The Lord pleads. He urges all who can to confront the large, overweight man. Uncle is his name. But a very soiled Uncle, as the red, white, and blue are hardly recognized on his garments. The Lord weeps openly. Can you hear His weeping? Sinful things of darkness that used to be hidden and rare are now celebrated openly. And the mouth of Hell grows wider each day.

Woe to those who plan iniquity to
Those who plot evil on their beds!
Micah 2:1

THE GREEN ROOM

I see a man at the door talking to human trafficking rescuers. They say they received word that some little children were being trafficked. The man who answered the door has a gun and acts like he's extremely concerned, claiming there aren't any here. The room is small, with green peeling paint and two doors. There is a dirty mattress in the corner and an old wooden chair; otherwise, the room is bare. The rescuers leave, determining they must've been wrong. However, they were not mistaken; they were right—the little girls were there and were quickly moved. The gatekeeper is a liar.

Lord, expose this operation! Bring strong, persistent people who will hear Your voice and will not give up. Many pass through this room where horrors unfold. Father, cover the innocent with your angels! Assign an angel to every single one of them and lead them safely home.

Fear not, for I have redeemed you; I have called you by name, you are mine.
Isaiah 43:1

THE NO NAMES

Lord, send workers into this plentiful harvest to rescue these little girls who don't have names, so no one is looking for them. They might have had names at one time, but now that they have been sold, they are referred to by the price at which they were sold. They are distinguished from others by the lusts of men who desire a specific hair color, body shape, or eye color, yet they remain nameless. But they have faces and hearts that the Lord knows, created, and loves. He weeps with great sobs at what man has done with His blessings through the gift of children.

The men who commit crimes against these children will not go unpunished. The Lord Himself feels the tears of the little Roses. He cries with them. He sees. Please, see His heart! Say yes to going into the harvest to rescue these little ones. It will not feel like a challenging assignment in Heaven.

And the very hairs on your head are all numbered. So don't be afraid; you are more valuable to God than a whole flock of sparrows.
Luke 12:27

DISPENSING OF SOULS

Outside of a room used for the dispensing of souls, I see a meter that takes money. A dollar amount appears, and then they're granted entrance like attending a concert. The dollar amount keeps going up as each young girl is herded through. There's no way back once they are admitted. Some of the little girls try to run before they get there, but they're constantly caught because they're little, and large, rough hands grab them. This is a private place that no one sees. It is heavily guarded, hidden down a country road with barricaded gates. The children are then put on a bus, or they board a plane, sometimes with their handlers, sometimes not. They are taken to different cities. Their little eyes are dead. Scared to death. Afraid to have emotions or cry. But their hearts cry to Jesus. Please minister to them, Holy Spirit, go to these little girls. Send an angel to each little girl.

The girls must be rescued from this room before they pass through the processing gate. To a sinful man filled with demons, they will forever be identified by the dollar amount they bring. Man's heart is indeed dark, but the Lord is greater, and He is sending light. He is calling for people who will trust Him and be strong in Him. Pray, people, pray!

When Jesus spoke again to the people, he said, "I am the light of the world. Whoever follows me will never walk in darkness but will have the light of life."
John 8:12

HELL TO PAY

It's hard to believe the horror of what is happening in our midst. Children are bought and sold so their organs can be harvested. Little souls, created to love and give love, are being used and abused for money.

The price is high for those who partake in these atrocities. The Lord sees, and this deed will not go unpunished. Even though the money flows, the day is coming when there will be no more money, and the soul of the criminal will be required. Here is where money cannot save you. Here is where the penalty for this sin against the God who created these little ones in His image will be known. So great will be the eternal pain of the perpetrators of these crimes that they will curse the day they came into the world. What has been done to the innocent child will be done to them. There will be no escape. No end to the punishment. Turn to the Lord now. Confess. Get out. Serve the Lord. Rescue the children and live. If you do not, there will be hell to pay forever and ever.

Father, save both the innocent and the guilty. May they find you while there is still a chance.

And he said to his disciples,
temptations to sin are sure to
come, but woe to the one through
whom they come! It would be
better for him if a millstone were
hung around his neck and he
were cast into the sea than he
should cause one of these little
ones to sin.
Luke 17:1-2

SO MANY MISSING

The Lord walks the earth in search of children. He hears their cries. Do you? Will you? He knows where they are and what their names are. He knows how old they are, what country they are from, and who their families are. He knows all. Will you join Him as He walks, weeping for the little ones? You are His body on earth now. He is calling, calling, calling for those who know Him to go forth into the darkness, the alleyways, the caves, and the hidden rooms. He is asking you to venture into basements, office buildings, and the homes of the rich and powerful and the poor to rescue these little souls. He loves them! Died for them. If you say yes, His angels will go with you and protect you. You need not fear. Ask Him to show you the things that break His heart, and you will see the little ones who are weeping for a God they may not know yet. Will you be the one?

For he will command his angels concerning you to guard you in all your ways.
Psalms 91:11

BROKEN HEARTS

I see the fathers and mothers. I observe grandpas and grandmas weeping before the Lord, lamenting that their child is gone, and no one knows where. The government refuses to acknowledge that this is happening. They pretend to close their eyes to what is right in front of them. The money is too lucrative. Blame is placed on those trying to save the children who are missing. Satan has descended to earth in a new and haunting way, and many follow him. At one time, they would have been horrified by the atrocities before them, but no more. Their hearts have been taken over by evil, and they are now the servants of the devil. And they think it is okay. Such deception! But the Lord sees and hears the cries of the little Roses. And he is getting ready to act.

Stand firm, servants of the Lord! Your God is on the throne, and His judgment will be swift and harsh for all who have sinned against one of these little ones. Angels carry the babies who are broken into His presence, where they will no longer hurt or cry alone. They are healed and loved and have forgotten all the pain they endured at the hands of evil men. But those who committed the crimes against them will never forget. Nor will their pain ever end.

But as for those whose hearts pursue their desire for abhorrent acts and detestable practices, I will bring their conduct down on their own heads. This is the declaration of the Lord GOD.
Ezekiel 11:21

To whom does your soul belong

Selfishness is deeply embedded in man's heart. Daily, man nurtures this selfishness, dominated by a desire for wealth, power, and status, crushing the delicate Roses intended to enrich the world. Many hearts have become cold and hardened. Sin flourishes, as the fruit of the womb is despised rather than cherished. Humanity has reached its lowest point, and the world's weak suffer due to this indifference and sin.

Humankind has distanced itself from God's heart, transforming the garden of Roses into a site of bloodshed and illicit wealth from the sale of body parts to the highest bidder.

God will not remain silent forever! He observes and records which side each aligns with. While Satan cannot create, he exploits what God has made, dismissing it as worthless and leading to its destruction. Pay attention! Which side are you on? Decide carefully, for eternity is everlasting.

Do not be deceived: God cannot be mocked. A man reaps what he sows. Whoever sows to please their flesh, from the flesh will reap destruction; whoever sows to please the Spirit, from the Spirit will reap eternal life.
Galatians 6:7-8

Silent bystanders

No longer can you be silent. You who see but do not speak. You who hurt for the victims but refuse to bring the guilty before the judge. Do you think that God will excuse your complacency? He has you where you are for a specific purpose. It is not to ignore the atrocities done to those made in His image. Others before you have also suffered greatly for speaking the truth. Soon, the judge of your life will be at the door on the night your soul is required of you, and you will give an account for why you did nothing.

The cries haunt you for a reason. Children are going missing because they were sold for money and the pleasure of men. If you know this, you are accountable for doing something while you are still in the body here on planet Earth. Speak up! The Lord and all the angels of Heaven are on your side. They will gird you up. Your home in Heaven is safe and secure, so do not fear to fight the good fight of faith now. A helpless one is waiting and weeping before the Lord to be rescued. Will you hear and help?

If anyone knows the good they ought to do and doesn't do it, it is sin for them.

James 4:17

HE WANTS TO ANSWER THROUGH YOU

There is a darkness that exists behind closed doors. Young girls are being lied to, ripped from their childhood, forced to grow up as victims of black hearts driven by greed and sold for a pittance, with no regard for their souls as they rob, kill, and destroy, working the works of the devil. Girls in pain, cold, and afraid, think no one sees, no one cares.

There is a light that overcomes as valiant soldiers of the cross go forth to the streets, fighting for the freedom of the soul God came to save, illuminating the darkness with His presence, not fearing those who kill the body but cannot kill the soul—knowing that there is nothing covered that will not be revealed or hidden that will not be known. Rescuing the helpless, trusting the greater One who sees and hears the cries of those still in slavery. Dark dungeon doors break open wide when you answer the cries of the little ones with no voice, no choice.

He wants to answer through you.

"He does not forget the cry of the afflicted.
Psalm 9:12

TUNNEL OF DEATH

The Lord sees you, worker of iniquity! You fool! Tonight, your soul will be required of you! What you have done to others will be done to you a hundredfold for all eternity. You will never not hear the cries of the babies you tortured. You will never forget how you laughed at their pain. Forever, you will see the pain in the eyes of the children you closed your heart to. Children made in God's image! Did you think He did not see or care? In your ignorance and lust, you destroyed the children, and now He shall kill you in hell's fire. He will arise and come to the rescue of those in cages and dark tunnels that were hidden to be sold to make the rich richer. There is a hell, and there is a judgment, and now it is too late for you. There was a price for your soul that Jesus paid in full, but you refused. And now you will know just how much it costs you. Yet His chosen Roses will know peace, safety, and joy for all eternity, while you suffer agony upon agony forever and ever.

*For there is nothing hidden
that will not be disclosed, and
nothing concealed that will not
be known or brought out into
the open.*
Luke 8:17

GOD SEES THE HEART

God sees not as man sees, for He knows the heart. It matters not that you are esteemed on a social media platform or that you have many followers because you sing well, can play a sport, are clever in your opinions, or have a talk show. He sees what lies beneath all that. And on the day the music fades and your fans are nowhere to be found, you will meet the God who created you for His glory. You will regret your choices to build your glory and derive your worth from man's worship of you. He knows how you lusted for more fame, money, and power, and how that turned to sin and the murder of babies that He gave to be a blessing. Your children, who never saw the light of this world, are with me now, but you will never know them. You choose the way of sin, hell, and the grave, and forever that is where you will be. It is too late, and your fans will worship you no more.

Then he will say to those on his left, "Depart from me, you who are cursed, into the eternal fire prepared for the devil and his angels."
Matthew 25:41

GO IN MY NAME

Do you not know that nothing you do for the Lord is wasted? Do you not understand that He is ready to give you more than you have given to Him in answering the cry of His heart to go into the dark alleys, tunnels, basements, apartments, and wealthy homes, and to rescue the little ones in His name and for His glory? Why do you fear when His angels go with you? Why do you tremble for your life when an eternal life of perfection is waiting for you? Why do you hide away to protect yourself when you cannot shield yourself from dying? Go now! Go in His name! Hurry! The children cry out to God, who made them. Come quickly and free them from the sinful lusts of man. On the day when the Lord will reward every man for what he has done, He will judge according to the motives of the heart and ask you, "Did you try to rescue? Did you go in My name? Did you go unafraid because I was with you?" You will not regret going. But you will regret staying.

"What, then, shall we say in response to these things? If God is for us, who can be against us?
Romans 8:31

HE WILL SHOW YOU

God says to remember what He has done! Remember Abraham; he set out not knowing where he was going. Likewise, He shows you the path to take. And He will direct whom you talk to and what you say. God will uncover what is hidden and expose the sin that is covered up. Has He not done this for you before? Can you believe He will do it again? Many are like you—going when He says go, not knowing where to go or what to do upon arrival. Isn't His presence with you enough? I know you feel weak. He is your strength. You are afraid. He is your peace and calm in any storm. On that great and terrible day of the Lord, you will rejoice that I have rescued you from eternal fire, so go now, knowing I will lead you safely home. What of the babies who have no home on earth? Can you answer their cries? Ask, and you shall receive. Ask to see, and you shall see. Constantly, their cries reach His heart. Their tears wet His face. Will you go for Him?

By faith, Abraham obeyed when
he was called to go out to a place
that he was to receive as an
inheritance. And he went out
not knowing where he
was going.
Hebrews 11:8

FOR ONLY ONE

There is too much evil to make a difference, you say. But will you try to bring the light? Will you pray? Even if one soul is redeemed, it will be rewarded a thousand times over in Heaven. It will be worth it even if just one life is saved and pulled from hell's fires. Pray for your enemies. Jesus died for them as well as you. He loves them, too, and will speak to them, and they will remember the day they refused Him and His forgiveness. They will never say that they did not know. Pray so they will see that they are making an eternal choice to continue the works of darkness and reap hell and death, or life and joy forever in Jesus. If one person does the will of satan and is set free, many will also be saved. Remember, Jesus looked at those who were crucifying Him and said, "Father, forgive them, for they know not what they do." Sin blinds us. Pray for the freedom of workers in the darkness as well.

For God so loved the world that He gave His only begotten Son, that whoever believes in Him will not perish but have everlasting life.
John 3:16

HE HEARS THEM

Jesus never overlooks the cries of the humble and innocent—the hurt and abandoned who are treated like refuse. Children instinctively reach out to God for help. The act of discarding these innocent beings as if they were waste plunges the soul into a state of moral decay. While the offenders escape punishment, the children are seen as undeserving of life. These small, beloved children, resembling their parents, enter this world for profit rather than to experience or give love, their true purpose defined by God's perfect design. By turning away from His blessings, one also turns away from the Giver. The heart becomes hardened, transformed as it descends into a darkness that is difficult to break free from. However, beware of those who assert that women should have control over their own bodies and the right to end the lives of children with separate DNA; they will face a far worse eternal consequence. And when they reach out, no one will answer.

For you will be treated as you treat others. The standard you use in judging is the standard by which you will be judged.
Matthew 7:2

DAY AFTER DAY

Day after day, they wait. They remember their mothers and fathers and the love they provided. Stomachs ache for food, and hearts yearn for love and care. But instead, they are met with rough hands that hurt deeply. Words can be soft and gentle at times, but they quickly become cruel and hateful. It's a nightmare from which they cannot wake. Endless crying follows, then the tears stop, for they discover that tears only bring more abuse and more pain. Thus, the strong ones learn to pretend. The weak ones are abused to death and then often further victimized by men filled with demons from hell.

There is a God who sees and waits day after day for someone to venture where only the strong and brave can go. To rescue those from the pits of man's creation, fueled by an insatiable lust to control and abuse. Day after day, the babies cry, but no one comes to save them. They are broken, hidden, kicked, and hurt again and again. They forget their names, their friends, and the toys they have played with before. They forget love, but God will take the little ones home, and His love will heal them. They shall play and be happy again in His home. Woe to the man who harms one of these little ones! You will never be satisfied again, nor will you be fed or treated with love and compassion. When your soul leaves your body, you will be in dark solitude forever, and your pain will never end.

For You formed my inmost being; You knit me together in my mother's womb.
Psalm 139: 13

An account must be given

Many are silent in the face of horror as little ones are sold and used. Many support the perpetrators of this heinous crime. On that Day of Judgment, you will not be found innocent! It has been placed in your hands to set the captives free and bring the children to a place of safety, but you refused. You feared the disapproval of man. You listened to the voice of the enemy, who hates the children made in the image of God. He heard every unspoken word. He knows of the time when you had great influence and could have spoken up, allowing the lost children to be found and brought to safety. Blood is on your hands! You will have no excuse on that day when the books of your deeds are brought forth. Now you shall reap what you sowed. What you neglected to bring to the world's attention will now be done to you in darkness and eternal torment. And you will never forget that you once had a choice and you chose wrong.

Your nakedness will be uncovered,
Your shame also will be exposed.
I will take vengeance and will
not spare a man.
Isaiah 47:3

Who did you vote for?

Man is quick to complain about injustices, yet few do anything about them. Too many are looking for a perfect man or woman to take the highest seat in the land. Yet, they do not even esteem the person who promised to end the murder of the innocents—the man who could put an end to the butchering of babies and children being sold and abused. But because the person they see is not perfect, they assume he is not God's chosen man for this time.

Such arrogance! Such idolatry. Do they not know there is no perfect person? All are imperfect. God uses the imperfect individual and always has. Too many did not ask Him for advice. They played God and assumed what He would say. Fools! So they stayed home and did not vote for the person He had picked to lead and stop the pain of His little ones. They have proven themselves unfit to be of any significant benefit in God's kingdom. Acting like children who are still mentally and spiritually dependent on milk when meat is before them. His strongest ones are those who seek His face and then judge.

Such arrogance! Such idolatry. Do they not know there is no perfect person? All are imperfect. God uses the imperfect individual and always has. Too many did not ask Him for advice. They played God and assumed what He would say. Fools! So they stayed home and did not vote for the person He had picked to lead and stop the pain of His little ones. They have proven themselves unfit to be of any significant benefit in God's kingdom, acting like children who are still mentally and spiritually dependent on milk when meat is before them. His strongest ones are those who seek His face and then judge and act accurately after He directs.

They built the high places of Baal in the Valley of the Son of Hinnom, to offer up their sons and daughters to Molech, though I did not command them, nor did it enter into my mind, that they should do this abomination.

Jeremiah 2:35

MAN IS BEING FOOLED

What a profound sorrow awaits those who think that simply making choices and changes in life will grant them freedom in the future. Fools! It is appointed for man to die once and then comes judgment. When the last breath is drawn on earth, the soul continues in another realm—one where flesh and blood cannot enter. An unwise person believes he can choose not to experience hell once he is there. He thinks he can negotiate with the Almighty, but he cannot. Satan has deceived the sinner, convincing him that hell won't be so terrible and that it will eventually end. "Live today, oh human," he whispers. "*Indulge your flesh as it desires! Be free and reshape your God-given identity into whatever you choose. Engage with whoever and whatever you want. There is no reckoning day. Unwanted pregnancy? Just rid yourself of it!*" This is wrong! God is not mocked. Whatever a man sows, that he will reap.

The King will reply, 'Truly I tell you, whatever you did for one of the least of these brothers and sisters of mine, you did for me.'
Matthew 25:40

Obsessed with pleasure

Believing your earthly pleasures are everlasting is a fatal error! You engage in buying and selling, yet your heart remains empty. Children weep in the chilling darkness of horror, while you focus on accumulating more possessions.

Ask Jesus what breaks His heart. Listen. Follow His guidance, and you will discover joy for all time.

One child at a time. One heart saved at a time. He doesn't ask you to save the entire world, but rather to see the world He came to redeem with fresh eyes. He died for everyone, so the broken could be healed, and all could find hope, and know joy, peace, and love forever. Allow Him to guide you. Seek His heart in everything. He will reveal how to live, and you will experience lasting pleasure and peace. We were made for Him.

You will show me the way of life,
granting me the joy of your
presence and the pleasures of
living with you forever.
Psalm 16:11

Pray His will

God views things differently than man does. He understands what a person can become, fully recognizing their shortcomings. He calls upon a soul, purifying it as it is presented to Him. He searches and discovers. Nothing is beyond His power. Many people assess and appreciate the actions of a person in authority and with considerable influence, even when they contribute nothing to God's kingdom.

Step forward, heed His call, and venture into the darkness! He is by your side. The light of Jesus within you will shine and reveal the darkness, facilitating healing. He perceives everything and will judge the unseen in due time. All will be disclosed. Approach His light. Request to see what He sees.

You are the light of the world. A city located on a hill cannot be hidden. People do not light a lamp and put it under a basket but on a lampstand, and it gives light to all in the house.
Matthew 5:14-16

You say times have changed

Yes, the world has transformed, but He remains unchanged. He brings life to the womb and has a purpose for each child. No child is a mistake. Humans may act as if they determine which infants will survive or perish. But can clay mold itself into a pot? He is the one who grants and takes away life.

Humanity is meant to be the guardian of the gift of children. It is a blessing from His hands. This blessing signifies His desire for humanity to endure and populate the earth. How arrogant for a man, whose breath could vanish in an instant, to assess the value of another human life! Judgment is reserved for those who disregard a soul that He formed in His likeness.

*Come now, you rich, weep and
howl for the miseries that are
coming upon you. Your riches
have rotted and your garments
are moth-eaten. Your gold and
silver have corroded, and their
corrosion will be evidence
against you and will eat your
flesh like fire.
James 5:1-20*

DEMONS OF OLD HAVE SEDUCED YOU

Your minds have become clouded as you follow the voices ignited by hell's flames. Yet, you do not seek the Lord's help to escape the dark grasp of hell that holds you captive. Instead, you ensnare others in the same way you are trapped. But the innocent ones, the victims, will be placed in the Lord's protection. Soon, you will cease to torment them, but you will suffer for your sins against the children for all eternity. You ignored God's voice, despite His many messengers. Greed filled your heart. Wealth that will perish alongside you in the fires of punishment. Did you believe God was unaware? Or indifferent? Soon, you will realize how mistaken you are. And you will never forget the countless opportunities He provided for you to turn to Him and confess.

Come now, let us reason together," says the LORD. "Though your sins are like scarlet, they will be as white as snow; though they are as red as crimson, they will become like wool.

Isaiah 1:18

YOU HAVE SOLD YOUR SOUL FOR A FEELING

Your craving for short-lived pleasures has ensnared you. They are merely momentary gains achieved at the cost of a child's life, which will never justify the loss. Soon, you will understand the actual price you have paid.

Yet, He will rescue the children from their abusers, but you refuse to accept salvation; you must admit your faults and renounce the desires that wage war on your soul, as they evoke the very demons of hell. However, if you call upon Him now, He will aid you. It is imperative to act immediately, for uncertainty looms over your tomorrows.

Because if you acknowledge and confess with your mouth that Jesus is Lord [recognizing His power, authority, and majesty as God] and believe in your heart that God raised Him from the dead, you will be saved.

Matthew 10:18

PART II
HEALING

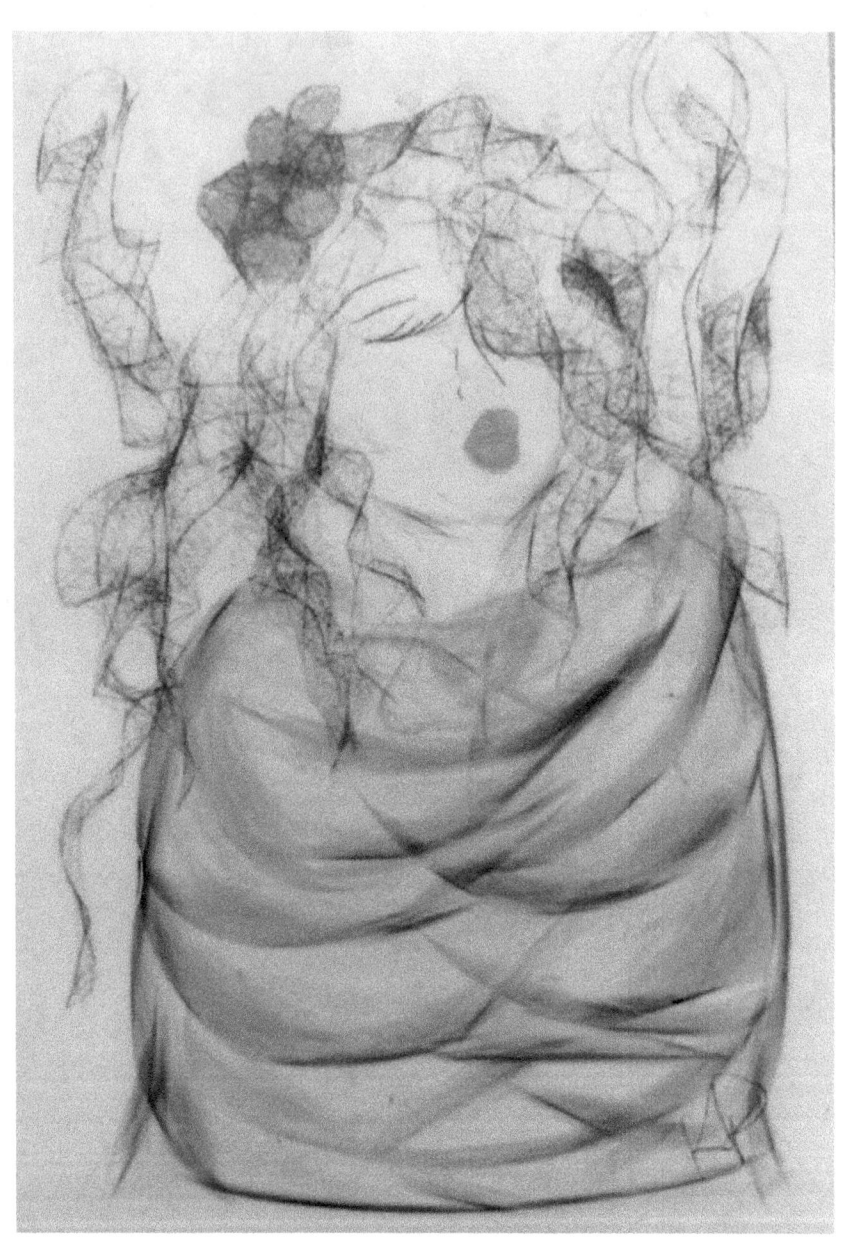

He heals the brokenhearted and binds up their wounds.
– Psalm 147:3

I HAVE YOUR BABY SAFE WITH ME

Jesus sees your heart and knows that it is breaking for the baby you were never able to hold in your arms. If you had a choice in the decision of whether your baby could live or die, He would forgive you for taking his life if you asked. He understands all the dynamics at work that led you to make that decision, and He wants you to know that He will turn it all to your good! Your precious child is safe with Jesus, happy and whole, with no ill feelings towards you. Babies are born in the Lord's heart before they are planted in the womb, and the Lord receives them back to Himself.

Come to Him and accept His salvation, and you will be reunited with your babies in eternity. This time, you will see their faces, hold them in your arms, and know the love they can give. You will weep for having missed this opportunity on earth. But in an instant, all pain will disappear, and the future will unfold before you. Eternity will be full of joy as you both grow and love together. He will restore and forgive, and all will be well.

So, know Him now. He is here. Come to Him with your brokenness and receive the hope that He longs to give you. Joy is on the way!

Jesus said, "Let the little children come to me, and do not hinder them, for the kingdom of heaven belongs to such as these."
Matthew 19:14

WHEN YOUR HEART IS BREAKING

You are overwhelmed, tormented by what you cannot control. Your grown child is aborting your granddaughter! You are reacting from the shock. He weeps with you. As your heart holds this baby in your arms, He has you in His embrace. Know that the life of this child is never truly gone, for she will come to live with God immediately. No more pain will touch her. She will be safe, healed, and whole. You will see her with your own eyes, not just in your spirit. She will be all you imagined her to be. Give her a name—a lovely name with much meaning for you. He will call her by that name, and so will you when you meet. That day and time are all arranged in the great and glorious hereafter, when all will be healed, and all tears will be wiped away.

Do not resent your daughter for the choice she made. She had no idea that this child would be an incredible blessing for her. Instead, pray for her, for her heart will long for the child she never held for the rest of her days on earth. She will need you in a whole new way, even if she never speaks of her loss. Call on the Lord, and He will be there.

And the prayer of faith will save the one who is sick, and the Lord will raise him up. And if he has committed sins, he will be forgiven.
James 5:15

HOW MANY HAVE YOU LOST?

Horrible things happened to you. Events were out of your control, and you suffered greatly at the hands of those stronger than you. They took what was not theirs and kept taking until you had nothing left inside. He understands emptiness, for He, too, was emptied when He died on the cross.

He, too, loved greatly and still does. Please know that what you lost will be restored to you. Let Him into that spot in your soul. Weep out the great pain of abuse, and He will weep with you.

Then, on some great and glorious day, your pain will be forgotten, and you will be healed. You shall see life where there once was only death.

Do not take revenge, my dear friends, but leave room for God's wrath, for it is written: "It is mine to avenge; I will repay," says the Lord.

Romans 12:19

WHEN YOU CAN'T FORGET WHAT WAS DONE TO YOU

My dear one, Jesus, the one who loves you, is here. He knows all and sees all. He understands that it can be hard to forget the pain inflicted upon you. Those who did not represent Him harmed you. The pain ran deep, often consuming you to the point that you could not separate who you truly are from what the abuse did to you and how it made you become. He can restore your soul! Jesus was wounded for the very pain you feel now. Even though you felt alone, you were not alone. He anticipated the day you would see Him as the One who loved you with an everlasting love. Before time began, He loved you. Let Him reach in and heal the hurt and make you new.

And he said to her,
"Daughter, your faith has
made you well; go in peace."
Luke 8:48

You honor Jesus with your faith

You have always sought Jesus, even when the pain was great and you did not understand, and this pleased His heart. You called out to Him during your abuse, knowing He heard you. Now the time has come for your healing. Jesus will be gentle, though the waves of memory will be intense. Afterwards, the pace will be sweet. As the gushing pain pours forth, know that He has planted special people in your path who will help you heal and bloom as the beautiful Rose you have always been. You have cried out in faith, and restoration will be known. You will go into your final days with praise on your lips for what He has done.

He will wipe away every tear from their eyes, and death shall be no more, neither shall there be mourning, nor crying, nor pain anymore, for the former things have passed away.
Revelation 21:4

WHEN THE WEEPING WILL NOT STOP

Oh, my child, Jesus understands! The wounds run deep. The memories haunt your sleep and torment your days. He is here! A day will come when you will no longer remember the pain. You will no longer live in fear of a knock at your door or a face you see in a crowd. Your sleep will be sweet, and a song will be on your lips when you rise. That day and time are kept safe in His keeping. Your joy shall never end. Until then, know Jesus holds your hand and will bring you safely home. Every day, He waits until you can embrace him forever in Heaven.

The day draws near when you will be home for all eternity. All pain will have been erased, and weeping will be a thing of the past. Until then, Jesus holds you and will carry you. Even if you do not feel Him there, He is there, and soon you will see.

*Be gracious to me, O Lord,
for I am languishing; heal me,
O Lord, for my bones are
troubled.
Psalm 6:2*

WHEN PAIN LINGERS

Child of the King, He understands how the pain lingers, how dreams haunt you even in the daylight. He carries this burden on His body and seeks to reach out and heal you. Please understand that sometimes healing comes in stages, as you can surrender yourself to Jesus. He has placed helpers in your path to guide you through painful memories and heal you there. Do not fear—He goes before you and has taken up your case in the courts of heaven. It has been determined that you are loved eternally, and His compassion for you will never end.

He was despised and rejected by men, a man of sorrows and acquainted with grief; and as one from whom men hide their faces, he was despised, and we esteemed him not. Surely he has borne our griefs and carried our sorrows; yet we esteemed him stricken, smitten by God, and afflicted. But he was pierced for our transgressions; he was crushed for our iniquities; upon him was the chastisement that brought us peace, and with his wounds we are healed.

Isaiah 53:1-12

SURVIVED BUT BARELY ALIVE

They insist you should feel grateful for your rescue and freedom from your abusers. They advise you to forgive and forget, to move on, and to embrace life. Yet, you struggle to do so. Their faces haunt you when you close your eyes. The pain resonates in your body and spirit, as if the bleeding will never cease. Though you seem fine on the surface, you are deeply wounded within your soul. Memories that won't let go haunt you day and night. You are alive, but on most days, you can barely rise or move. He, too, suffered greatly. Left to die alone. He, too, stood bare before the world, unjustly whipped and beaten.

Continue to seek God when the pain becomes unmanageable, when no one else is equipped to hear you truly. Approach Him, and you will soon realize that He carries you now, heals your wounds, and offers you a new life—a fresh beginning. It is not too late. He loves you.

And they were bringing even their babies to Him so that He would touch them, but when the disciples saw it, they began rebuking them. But Jesus called for them, saying, "Permit the children to come to Me, and do not hinder them, for the kingdom of God belongs to such as these. Truly I say to you, whoever does not receive the kingdom of God like a child will not enter it at all."

Luke 18:15-17

COME AS YOU ARE

Do you ever feel like a child because you didn't feel loved or wanted? And today, do you still feel the emptiness from the love you never received? The affirmation that should have been there wasn't, and now you're looking for a place to connect your soul so you can be revitalized and loved in a way you never experienced before.

Come to Jesus. Just as you are now. Fragile. Damaged. Isolated. Approach Him in your pain, like a child lacking love, whose innocence was taken by monsters who harmed you deeply, leaving behind scars that seem impossible to erase.

He will restore your spirit, and one day, the pain and trauma will fade from your memory. Come to Him as you are in this moment, and He will make you whole again. It is possible to be loved and treasured as you always deserved. You are eternally loved, even amidst your doubt. He awaits with open arms, ready to embrace you.

Bless the Lord, O my soul,
And forget not all his benefits,
who forgives all your iniquity,
who heals all your diseases.
Psalm 103:2-3

It's okay if you do not feel it.

It's perfectly normal to feel broken, wounded, and isolated. Your emotions are valid, and God comprehends them. He values your sacrifice of praise, even when expressing it feels too painful. When you feel angry because of the pain He allowed, He understands, and finds beauty in your praise, especially when it is hard to trust. Give your will over to him and ask for His heart for you. He empathizes with the anguish of your soul during those lonely nights when you feel miserable, as though your soul has been violently torn from your body and trampled by satan and his armies of demons.

Remember, His love surpasses satan's hatred. One day, he will be vanquished, but you will be cherished, restored, and joyful in God's eternal Kingdom of love. Come and witness this; it is almost prepared for you. There, you will praise freely, with no recollection of the pain you suffered. Instead, you will remember only the love He had for you, which saved you and brought you into eternal life with Him.

*The Lord sustains him on his
sickbed; in his illness, you restore
him to full health.*
Psalm 41:3

Your life is not over.

There is a future filled with hope and joy waiting for you. Who told you that you were doomed to die? Who told you that God cannot heal you and give you a new life? He can do what man cannot do. Can you trust Him?

I understand that people have hurt you deeply, and you are afraid to trust a man, but Jesus is not like the men of earth who have been born into sin. He is entirely different, full of love, forgiveness, and compassion. Jesus comes in when everyone else leaves. He has plans for you that are for good and not for evil, to give you a future and a hope. Yes, good plans for you!

"I know the plans I have for you," says the Lord, "plans to prosper you and not to harm you, plans to give you hope and a future."
Jeremiah 29:11

Your healing is not a distant dream.

The Lord wants all who trust in Him for healing to know that soon, the desert of your life will blossom like a rose. This metaphor of a desert blooming like a rose symbolizes the transformation and beauty that God can bring to our lives, even during the most barren and desolate times. A rose that was always loved and planned for, even though man rejected it. Even though it was trampled, forgotten, wounded, and broken into a thousand little pieces, soon, your eyes shall see the land filled with the new life of beautiful red roses. Roses that grew and blossomed in His heart. Soon, it will be here before you, and you will remember nothing but what you see before you. He shall restore all.

The wilderness and the land will be glad; the desert will rejoice and blossom like a rose.

Isaiah 35:1 1

ABOUT THE AUTHOR

Lorene Masters is an accomplished poet and author of eleven books with a diverse background that enriches her literary works. Her books, such as *The Tin Trailer and Other Poems for the Hurting and the Hopeful*, *Chasing White Horses - Poetry for Women Who Love Too Much*, *The Women He Loved - Dramatic Monologues of Encounters with God*, and *Hungry Heart - How One Woman Found Love*, have garnered critical acclaim. Notably, *Hungry Heart* won the Grand Prize Award of the Inspiring Voices (Guideposts) Book Publishing Contest, a testament to her literary prowess.

When Roses Fall is not just a book; it's a call to action. It delves into the serious issue of sex trafficking, challenging readers to be a part of the light that shines in the overwhelming darkness of this global issue. *Words in the Wilderness - Letters to My Bride* offers short, encouraging devotions with Bible verses for meditation and prayer. *A Voice Was Seen - Visions of Eternity* is a fascinating account of her journey into the spiritual realm. It encourages us that an incredible world awaits followers of Jesus.

Lorene is an ordained pastor with the Foursquare Church, a prophetic intercessor, a radio personality for over 25 years, and an actress who performs original dramatic monologues for Christian meetings and retreats. She is also an eating disorder survivor, a sex trafficking awareness advocate, and a Lyme Disease survivor. Her passion for praying for others and providing encouragement is evident in her ministry outreaches. Her journey of resilience and determination is a testament to her strength and inspires many.

Lorene can be contacted at **Lorenemasters@gmail.com.**

www.ingramcontent.com/pod-product-compliance
Lightning Source LLC
Chambersburg PA
CBHW051924220626
47052CB00003B/568